YOUNG MASTERS
The Hidden Treasure

Written by Bunny Hull

Illustrations by Kye Fleming

Layout & Typography by James Suelflow

ISBN 0-9721478-8-8

Little Wisdom Series
© 2007 Dream A World®

www.dreamaworld.com

Butaan and Phylos often sat beneath the old oak tree discussing very important things.

"Why do you think people give you gifts for your birthday?" asked Phylos.

"Because they're happy you were born," said Butaan, handing Phylos a package with a big purple bow.

"Once I gave Aunt Saphinne some yellow flowers I grew myself," said Phylos.

"I'm happy she was born."

4

"Happy Birthday Phylos!" said Butaan.

Phylos smiled a wide smile and carefully opened the package.

There it was...
the most beautiful box kite.

"Oh Butaan, thank you!"

"You're welcome!"
said Butaan.

"And you know what else?
I don't think the gift is
the most important thing.
I think people give gifts
to remind us about the
hidden treasure."

"What hidden treasure?" asked Phylos.
"Is it buried somewhere?"

"Kind of...," said Butaan.

"Like a buried in the ground, in a treasure chest, kind of
   treasure?" asked Phylos.

"No," said Butaan, "but it's hidden somewhere you would
   never think to look..."

"Is it worth a lot of money?" asked Phylos, imagining what he might be able to buy if he found it.

"Oh it's worth much more than money," said Butaan.

"Well, where is it?" asked Phylos, "Is it something I can see?"

"It's something you can feel," said Butaan, "inside."

"What kind of feeling? asked Phylos.

"You know when your heart is so full of happiness it feels like a big balloon about ready to burst?" asked Butaan."

"Oh...that," sighed Phylos, watching his kite sail higher up into the sky. "Like what I'm feeling right now. I like that feeling."

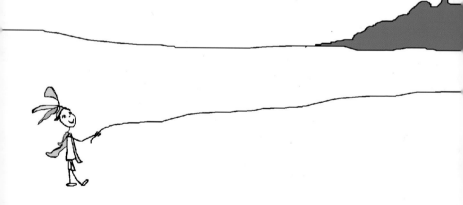

"Thank you, wind!"

11

"That's it!"
said Butaan,
"that's the
hidden treasure.
It's feeling thankful."

"I feel thankful when I hear birds sing," said Phylos.

"I feel thankful for the smell of fresh cut grass in the summer," said Butaan.

"I feel thankful for the sunrise every morning," said Phylos.

"I feel thankful for jelly sandwiches..." said Butaan.

"...and for my cat Oracle."

"Thank you planet earth," said Phylos,

"for giving us water and food and being a home
to so many different people and animals."

"Thank you ears," said Butaan,
"you let me hear music."

"Thank you eyes, you let me see a rainbow."

"I think we found the hidden treasure,"
said Phylos."

"There's always something to be thankful for
said Butaan.

"It makes my heart feel good," said Phylos, "just to say
thank you for everything."

"You know Phylos, the best gift I ever received is
having you for a friend," said Butaan. "Thank you."

Thank you for being here!

Download the song lyrics at **www.dreamaworld.com**

"Over The Sky & Under The Moon," "Everyday Is A Gift,"
"Doesn't It Make Your Feel Good," and "Circle of Appreciation"
written, produced and performed by Bunny Hull

"The Magic Eye" is read by Elayn J. Taylor

Flute: Diane Hsu * Guitars: Greg Poree & James Harrah * Trumpet: Lee Thomburg
Children's chorus: Los Angeles Elementary School;
Maria Castellanos, Crystal Overstreet, Tatiana Lozano, Jonathan Solis,
Rocio Canales and Adrienne Rivera; under the direction of Jack Burke

Oracle the Cat: Bailey Hull

Additional mixing, drums and percussion: Jeff Hull

Recorded and mixed by Bunny Hull at
Dream A World Studios, Los Angeles

Mastering: Dwarf Village Studios; Valley Village, CA

To all my beautiful friends and extended family… Thank you for your love and
support, especially IPA and Charlotte Sherman who listened every step of the way.

Bunny Hull – Writer, Producer

A resident of Los Angeles, California, Hull is a Grammy Award®-winning songwriter and recipient of over 20 Gold and Platinum albums, with songs that have appeared in films and on television which include *The Prince Of Egypt, Bruce Almighty, Sesame Street, Oprah, The Simpsons* and *Evan Almighty.*

In the world of children's books and music, Hull is the recipient of a Parents' Choice Award, Three National Parenting Publication Awards, two Dr. Toy Awards and a Parent's Guide To Children's Media Award. She is well-known for using music and the arts to inspire children to learn about positive aspects of life, self-image, diversity, relationships, and the importance of expressing their individuality.

Kye Fleming – Illustrator

A Nashville, Tennessee resident, Fleming comes from the music world where she has established a career as an award-winning songwriter; three time BMI Writer of the Year; and Grammy, CMA, ACM and Dove nominee. Other awards include Billboard Song of the Year and Nashville Songwriter Association International nominee for Hall of Fame.

Art is something that comes naturally, and her computerized characters emerged when Fleming purchased an iBook a few years ago. These drawings are created with AppleWorks, a finger and a track pad. "Young Masters" is Fleming's entry into the world of illustration. Personal philosophies: Motivation: fun; Inspiration: life; Perspiration: I don't believe in it; Advice: pet your cat.

Elayn J. Taylor – Saphinne, Our Storyteller

Elayn lives in Los Angeles and has appeared in film and on television including, *Bruce Almighty, Something's Gotta Give, Rules of Engagement, Dr. Doolittle 2, Sabrina, Strong Medicine, The Practice* and more. Her stage appearances include *Rose in Fences, Gem Of The Ocean* (L.A.), *Someplace Soft To Fall* (St. Paul), and *Joe Turner* (Houston).

Diane Hsu – Flute

Diane lives in Los Angeles and performed as a concerto soloist from the age of 11 with the Seattle Philharmonic Orchestra, the Northwest Chamber Orchestra, the University of Washington Symphony and has been a selected participant in Boston Univeristy's Tanglewood Institute. Also an actress, she has appeared on film and in television in *How Stella Got Her Groove Back, Snapdragon, Totally Blonde, James Bond: License To Kill, The West Wing, Family Matters, Sunset Beach, Bloodlines* and more.

Also available from Dream A World:

"The Friendship Seed"   "The Magic Eye"

"A Child's Spirit"   "Peace In Our Land"

"Creative World"   "Dream A World"

"Alphabet Affirmations"   "Happy Happy Kwanzaa"

www.dreamaworld.com